Bobbin

Bubble

by Kerrie Jane McCarthy

Jump on the white Hare
He will take you there
To Bobbin Bubble
where there's no trouble

Have some lunch with Elsie Crumpet
Or Hear Tempus on his Bottom Trumpet
Taste Betty's Homemade raisin Scones
or Help Prince Poggle find his Bone

Lily's tearoom serves hot toast
where Enri Batonz likes to boast
and Malcom wears his green canoe
They are all here, waiting ...just for you.

Come Fly With Me...

When my daughter Jenny was younger (but probably older than she would care to admit) she sat at the dinner table one evening and, with her eyes full of tears, asked "Mummy, is Santa real?".

I answered that " Yes, Santa is alive in your heart and your head" and this message has been at the forefront of our Christmases ever since. How I see it, we have two choices - choosing not to believe drains everything of its colour and makes everything feel flat. Believing makes everything bright and magical, so why would anyone choose not to believe? I would like you to apply this same rule when reading Bobbin Bubble. A little more Whimsy, nonsense and laughter would make the world a much nicer place.

May you never be too old to search the skies on Christmas eve.

Kerrie, a.k.a Mrs Bobbin xxxx

Teddy's Emporium.... the only shop specialising in "The Human need". In case you didn't know, all dogs are completely capable of knowing exactly what you need at any given moment (its science relating to the dog hairs they leave on your clothing... but I won't go into that now)

Teddy is in charge here, and he believes that all Human problems can be solved with a giggle... or possibly a trump. However, Teddy (being the tinker that he is) likes to give both of these out together, or sometimes mix them up. This is the reason why sometimes when you trump... you can't help but giggle and sometimes when you giggle... you can't help but trump.

Teddy, store manager, likes to fill the front of the shop with Doggy essentials- watermelon, squeaky toys and lots of biscuits. His favourite ways to cheer up his humans are: Wiping eye bogies on light coloured trousers, distributing dirty paw prints and impromptu zoomies

Ruby is the Trump manufacturer – her specialities are Egg, Beef, cheese and Chicken Tikka. Unfortunately, this does mean that she sometimes struggles with her "work/life balance" and cant help but let the trumps out at unfortunate times..... it's a small price to pay for her career. She used to be a ballerina... but after one incident, after eating a boiled egg, she became known as " The Badger Bum ballerina"

Boo Bear is a tricycle expert-
she spends the day pedalling
the trike around the Bubble,
delivering Teddy's order's of
Giggles and Trumps to all the
humans. At weekends though,
she is more famously known
as "Boo Bear the Brave" for
pedalling speeds of up to 90
miles per hour on "The Wall of
Death" at Mr Bobbin's Circus

Posey Pickle is new to the job
and is currently being trained
-so isn't quite in tune with her
doggy sensors yet. At the
moment though, she seems to
think that everyone needs " A
good Roast dinner and a
snooze"

<u>Ruby's Top Tip:</u>

"Always wear pants when
Pirouetting"

Elsie Crumpet can often be seen dawdling in the reduced section, of her local supermarket. She lives on out of date produce and hates any waste. Horrified that a week's shopping cost £17.

"Seventeen Pounds I ask you!" She repeats to all the shoppers at the checkout

Food combinations at meal times are often interesting. Boiled onion with a sprinkling of cheese or to treat herself (and Prince Poggle) she makes Chicken Surprise- But due to the cost of Chicken these days she swaps it for her favourite ingredient..... Onions.

Monday......A whole boiled onion with a small sprinkling of cheese

Tuesday.....Onion soup

Wednesday.....French onion soup (same soup as yesterday but with cheese on toast- must use Brie, its far more continental)

Thursday.....Pickled onion puree with sardines

Friday.....Chicken Surprise—chicken is too expensive these days so replace it with extra onions

Saturday.....Cheese pie with onion julienne

Sunday.....Roast Haggis with an Onion reduction

Snacks-prepare Loaded onion skins.- stuff the skin of the onion with last weeks leftovers and bake for 20 mins

Grand Designs- the Deluded Edition

Elsie completely re-designed her "Travelling Apartment". Small space living is about being multi-functional. Her state of the art, eco-friendly, "al-fresco bathroom" in co-ordinating pink has done away with the need for expensive extractor fans, heating, taps or even a sink.

Pure genius

Kelvin Mclouder

♪♪

"Last Christmas I gave You my heart,
but the very next day, you gave it
away... This year, to save me from
tears , I'll give it to someone special"

♪♪

"Well Yes!" " Would that not have been a
good idea to start with" Elsie Crumpet
exclaimed to the radio, as she threw her
chocolate orange at it. She was listening
to Christmas "boogey anthems" for the
Over 50's and Physically Impaired
station... she had little time for romance.

Elsie Crumpet doesn't want to be under the mistletoe with anyone other than Prince Poggle. He's the love of her life.

These two really are just perfect together...she's bossy, has flatulence issues and never stops talking ....and he is stubborn, has absolutely no sense of smell and is completely tone deaf

After going missing at the annual New
Year's Party.... Miss Crumpet was found in
a rather undignified position in a plant pot
snoring like a wart hog in the greenhouse.
On waking she did manage a little wave to
her public whilst uttering something about
peasants and privacy ....completely
believing herself to be the Queen of
Denmark.

Mr Tempus Fugit, the man who keeps the time. Sadly, Tempus is not very bright, and thought he was going for a job as a lighthouse keeper. Well, I suppose to a Bunny, a Grandfather clock could look like a lighthouse (Yes, I am being kind).

Between you and I, he can't actually tell the time. He only got the job as Slack Alice, from Accounts, took a shine to him in his interview. His knowledge is limited, very limited.

He once shouted out at Quiz night, that Pontious Pilot was in the RAF and that if you "just stay on" the Eurostar, you can get to India. It had long since been his dream to live alone, to get away from the overcrowded burrow, and live an uncomplicated life were he did not have to excuse his Bottom Trumpet.

When Tempus got the job, Slack Alice told him

"There is some furniture in the Clock that will do for the time being..."

The only thing Tempus actually heard was ..."Time Bean" which he assumed was his new title. He now introduces himself as "Tempus Fugit, Time Bean."

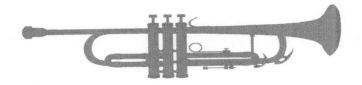

Tempus was very excited when he saw
that the local Sprout Group were
advertising for Trumpeters to perform
at the local church. To perform at the
Christmas Concert would be an
honour- the Wind Section, in
particular required immense
stamina.

At the audition, Tempus was
intrigued by Malcolm- the canoe
wearing trumpeter, who had the most
remarkable trumpet he had ever seen!

Malcolm and Tempus harmonized
beautifully through the final notes of
Silent Night. Tempus was amazed by
Malcom's ability to reach the high
notes- they even pulled the same facial
expression (one eye half closed and a
half smile, accompanied by the flush
of red cheeks)

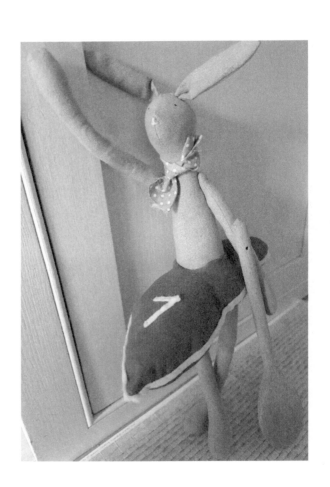

Malcolm didn't quite
get the message when
his Dad told him that
women like

"Sporty Men".

When they drained the local pool, Malcolm realised he could finally combine his two passions: Fashion and Sport. This was how "Canoeasize" was born. Impromptu dry land canoeing performed all over the bubble- most commonly, in the Doctors waiting area, in the loading bay at "Toys Were Us" and the freezer section in the local super market.

Until his students have graduated and earned their "Canoe pants", Malcom will not allow interaction with actual canoes and so they must improvise and create their own vessels. This Process takes approximately seven years.

(Please do not pay attention to Stanley in the back ground with his tomato, this will only encourage him)

Lily's tea rooms works purely on kindness. Do a kind deed and you get cake. Malcolm used to work at the tea rooms but due to his Canoe pants (and flatulence issues) things didn't quite work out.

Lily was very understanding of Malcolm's bottom trumpeting as her father had been the original grand S.P.R.O.U.T leader. Malcolms idea of tooting like a train to cover his parps merely drew attention to him......stopping fellow diners in their tracks.

On Fridays Lily offered the " Big Bottom Special" to the S.P.R.O.U.T group to give them stamina. This consisted of fried sprouts, cabbage and mashed potato with a side order of beans (known to you as Bubble and Squeak as that's exactly what happens after)

Stamina and

Practice make

Rippers

Out-loud

U keep

Trumpeting

Weigh in day at "Ditsy Dimble's Hungry Bellies slimming club" (which is always hosted in Lily's Tearooms). Ditsy didn't like to see so many sad faces every Thursday morning at weigh in. The bellies were rumbling so loudly that people couldn't hear Ditsy talking about how important it is to be happy too. So now Ditsy likes to bring along some homemade cakes and treats, some music and a bubble machine and they have a good giggle and a good old boogie. The slimming club has gone from strength to strength and is referred to in the bubble as the "Smiling club".

Major Enri Batonz (well that is his title this week) likes to spend his days in Lily's tea room. Sat in a cool corner, drinking cold green tea that he thinks is algae (then again, if you tasted it you would probably agree).

Enri likes to reminisce about his past and talk of his time at R. A.D .A and the medal he won for "Civilian Gallantry". His favourite stories are about the nervous years living in Pugh Fearnley Whittingstall's garden and his time spent as bass guitarist for Queen

Lily's Wall of Fame, or "Pool of Drool" as Enri jokingly refers to it. Each time Enri plays a new role, he gifts a new headshot to Lily. She has so many and now the wall is full....so she uses them as trays, filters on the extractor fan in the kitchen and has even used them to repair the tearoom roof.

This week Lily is trying a new method- buy a cappuccino and get a free headshot of Erni... Cappuccino sales are now down 100%.

Enri likes to discuss his colourful past with each and every customer. Unfortunately, Enri has a very, very poor memory. It is rumoured that he has genes that are very similar to a goldfish after his mother "went swimming in the wrong tank".

Enri's most notable career achievements are as follows....

SPAWN

Dumpy and Gabana

He was an aftershave
model for Dumpy and
Gabana

He played Tommy
Scooper in a Westend
production of
"Just Like That"

He was Captain Henry
Baton of the 5th Battalion
of the 7th area of the sea.

It is Reputed that Enri
makes his own
hats....but...

"Just because you haven't
heard of the HMS
Spaghetti, doesn't mean
it doesn't exist"

There was also an "adapted" Shakespearian Tribute which he directed, produced and starred in....

the One Man show "Romeo and Henriette"

He was also Major Henry Baton-Smith- he was highly decorated and notoriously "knew what he was doing with his weapon"

As Henrietta Garland, he starred in the Australian Outback production of "Wizard of Aus" but this was short lived as apparently he felt the conditions were unacceptable.... For a western frog, being constantly upside down put too much pressure on his acting abilities.

Enri sadly narrowly missed out on the starring role in the upcoming thriller called "Chameleon". A film about a master of disguise who can blend into any environment.

The Irony, for poor Enri is that the job that might have made him famous, is the job he never wants to discuss. He was formally the belt buckle for the runner Linfield Christy... but after misplacing one froggy foot and slipping during a promo-shoot, he became famous for all the wrong reasons.

Betty and Bitsy were discussing the new "Skinny Mini" bars they had seen in the supermarket...

" Oh Betty, do I seriously look like someone who eats Skinny Mini bars?" Bitsy laughed rubbing her belly

" Well, it could be worse.. I bought them ... and ate the whole box!" cried Betty

Last years bumper crop of
pumpkins were still a very sore
subject in the Bear house. For 27
days straight now the bear family
have eaten pumpkin in varying
forms..Pumpkin soup, pumpkin
pie, pumpkin roast, pumpkin and
chips. Mr Bear has even had it on
his sandwiches at work.

Today Mr Bear returned from work
early , mainly due to his work
colleagues demanding that his
office be fumigated. He walked
through the door into the kitchen,
saw the ingredients for the evening
meal on the table and made the
terrible mistake of saying:

"Not piggin' pumpkin again" just
a little bit too loud as he rubbed his
swollen little belly....

The spare bedding is now on the sofa....and Brenda (Mrs Bear) is in the bath with a massive bag of Rebels she's had hidden in the airing cupboard. Sadly they were a bit too close to the hot water tank and so have moulded into one large chocolatey treat , but that isn't stopping her eating it like a chocolatey corn on the cob.

Aunty Nellie, nobody is quite sure who's aunty she is, but every family function, wedding, Christening or dental extraction she is there. More often than not, Nellie attends these events with "the perfect gift"- Dance numbers performed to a range of her favourite "show tunes" in the same outfit that she wore on stage 40 years ago... despite the fact she has since gained 4 stone.

She will always be wearing shoes, she can hardly walk in and dressed up to the nines. Red feathers can often be seen peeking over the top of her handbag, as she still carries her show-girl headdress- keen for any opportunity to show off her moves.

In her twenties, Nellie was the most beautiful dancer on Broadway, but 30 years later, after one very fateful Christmas Party with the Show Girl Academy, where she drank a little too much Champagne and the buttons on her exhausted body suit gave way, she was turned away from the academy and forced to face a world without showbiz.

Luckily, at the time, she was still on good terms with the City's leading Cosmetic Dentist- Mr Edward Namel. She had often exclaimed that it was a real waste for the extracted teeth of the rich and Famous to be disposed of. So after her disgraceful exit from the Show Girl academy, she sank her savings into starting her own business, turning the teeth of the biggest stars in to Door Knockers- because who wouldn't want the teeth of their favourite stars hanging from their front doors?

The only problem with the deal she made with Mr Namel, was that she was not allowed to reveal the source of the teeth she bought - but here "Nellies Knockers" was born.

Roll up.....Roll up....Mr.Bobbin's
Circus is in town!
Prepare to see acts like you've never
seen before:

Master Teddy will enter riding a
White Wild Goose (well Big Brenda
who works as a Doctor's receptionist
Monday to Friday) and will
attempt to jump an ironing board
and a large tin of white
emulsion (matte, not silk)

Miss Ruby will attempt to dive 75
feet into a Tango bottle filled with
popcorn ...wearing only a pair of
70 denier support tights.

Not forgetting our star act...
Death defying bravery as Boo bear
the brave enters the Wall of Death
on her tricycle.

It was Posey Pickle's first
Bobbin Circus, so she was
given the job of handing out
the popcorn to the guests...
but poor little Posey found
the task to be very
overwhelming...

Elsie Sells food at the Bobbin Circus.

Her culinary delights include-

- The Circus " Four Onion special" – (Spring, fried, pickled and boiled)
- Whole onion pizza –
- Hot dogs with mustard- (no dogs)
- Hot dogs with Ketchup- (no dogs)
- Burgers- no burgs
- Cheese and Onion Pie
- Cheese and Onion Pasties
- Bread, butter and onion delight
- Bread and Onion pudding- a savoury twist on the popular "Bread and Butter pudding"

Next time you are at the Circus, school fete or Christmas Fair,

and you smell fried onions, you will just know that Elsie is there.

Prince Poggle's secret to Freedom... Is
Candyfloss. He wears this as hair, and this
allows him to move around "In -Cognito"

Prince Poggle plays a very important role in the Crumpet Culinary Enterprise. His Job is to lick all the onions on the pizzas, to ensure they stick. This is a role he has taken upon himself, he has never been asked to and he does it in secret.

His real love though, is the Toffee Apples- from the crunchy, juicy fruit right down to the stick (the very best part, of course). But as we all know... too many apples... too much trumpeting.

Elsie assumed, in her innocence, that by allowing Stanley to choose a big Pie from her stall, that she would discourage his usual antics...

...Elsie was
wrong...

You've heard of smoked kippers in Whitby? Guinness in Dublin? Oatcakes in Staffordshire? Well now we have Numpkin with the sweet pumpkin stall. When Numpkin realised he had extremely large pumpkins he decided to start his sweet pumpkin stall. He had no idea it would be so popular! But now Numpkin's pumpkins brings all of the bears to the yard.

Stanley thought that pushing his way to the front and "Bearing all" at Numpkin in his green mac might get him served quicker... Needless to say Stanley was promptly sent home.

And a word to the wise from Elsie Crumpet

"**Today,** Stanley has taught you all a **valuable lesson... pushing to the front of** the queue and revealing yourself, will **<u>NOT</u>** get you the sweet Pumpkins"

"Underpants...So why aren't" there Underknickers. This was Malcolm's thought of the day...The rest of the day he has been practicing the first three lines of "Santa Claus is coming to town" on his Bottom Trumpet.

Dear Readers,

Mrs Bobbin has instructed me to write this to explain my behaviour in this book as apparently it is very "inappropriate".

I hope that the intellectual readers of this book have been able to understand the true intent of my actions. But for those, like Mrs Bobbin, who have failed to understand, let me explain:

You have all read the stories of a certain yellow bear, plodding round the woods eating his weight in Honey, or perhaps you were more of a fan of the other bear- who like me, chose to wear nothing but a blue coat and fetching hat. They have both been adored for years, have had books, films and merchandise made about them... but here is me, wearing a much more sophisticated ensemble but I am scolded, mocked and hit with rolled up newspapers for being trouserless in public.

I am a simple bear and do not want for much.... but feel the lack of focus on me in this book was discriminatory of my clothing choices.... I would like you all to know, I am currently working on my own masterpiece that shall be titled either "A memoirs of a bare Bear" or "'Stanley put your trousers on'"

Mr Stanley Bear

This is a huge thank you to all the
wonderful creators and friends who have
helped me to bring Bobbin Bubble to life-
if you would like to buy some of your
own characters, please check out these
amazing Instagram accounts:

@sew_charming18
@jane.creelman
@flossie_and_boo
@pipfitzp
@bessieandbee.illustration

And a special thank you to baby Bobbin
and Mr Bobbin for believing in me.

Printed in Great Britain
by Amazon